THE STORY OF

THE

BETROTHED

SAVE THE STORY

Umberto Eco

ILLUSTRATED BY MARCO LORENZETTI

Translated by Stephen Sartarelli

PUSHKIN CHILDREN'S BOOKS

Pushkin Children's Books
71-75 Shelton Street
London, WC2H 9JQ

The Story of the Betrothed first published in Italian as *La storia de I Promessi Sposi*
© 2010 Gruppo Editoriale L'Espresso S.p.A
and © 2010 Umberto Eco. All rights reserved.

This edition published by Pushkin Children's Books in 2014

ISBN 978 1 782690 22 1

Set in Garamond Premier Pro by Tetragon, London

Printed and bound in Italy by Printer Trento SRL
on Munken Print Cream 115gsm

www.pushkinpress.com

THE STORY OF

THE
BETROTHED

One

Once upon a time there was…

"A king!" the smaller readers will say, accustomed as they are to fairy tales.

No siree. That's the way Pinocchio begins, and it's a beautiful fairy tale, but the story about to be told here is almost true. I say "almost" because the man who told it, Signor Alessandro, a Milanese noble with a nice face who looked a little like a sad horse and lived about 200 years ago, claimed he had found it written on some leaves of paper that today would be almost 400 years old, since the story takes place in sixteen-hundred and something.

So let's start again. Yes, here too, once upon a time there was a king, the king of Spain, though he doesn't appear in our story except from afar. But once upon this particular time there was in fact a fearful priest, so fearful that a shutter slamming in the wind was enough to make him pee his pants in fright. (Sorry for the somewhat vulgar expression, which I'm sure you never use, but in this case I can because our priest was really that fearful.)

How can that be? you may ask. Shouldn't a priest follow the precepts of the Gospel and be good, generous and brave in the defence of his flock? Don't we read nowadays about priests who have actually been murdered because they stood up to the Mafia and the Camorra? Well, yes, but the writer with the horse-face, though a good Christian, knew that men could be brave or fearful independently of their job requirements. And he also knew that, at the time, many became priests or friars (or nuns) not from any sense of vocation, and in a spirit of sacrifice, but because those were times of great hardship; and for a poor man, becoming a priest or friar (or a poor woman a nun) was a way to make sure that, while he might not exactly live it up for the rest of his life, he would not die of starvation. So it was certainly possible for someone only trying to get by to become a priest without paying much mind to the Gospels.

Those were hard times. The greater part of Lombardy, the region of Italy in which our story takes place, was under Spanish rule, which rested on the support of an assortment

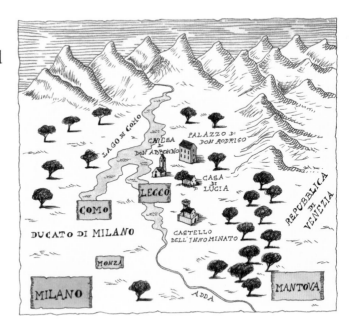

of Italian nobles great and small, who in return had licence to commit all manner of abuse. They often lived in Milan, but also in dark castles and little palaces perched high above towns and villages and protected by their bravoes.

Who were these bravoes? Today we would call them bodyguards, but be careful: they were real scoundrels guilty of every imaginable kind of wickedness. The petty nobles would hire them to save them from prison or the gallows, and in return they were ready to commit any sort of outrage their lords requested of them. Such acts were rarely between one lord and another, and usually between a nobleman and some poor people.

A bravo was easy to spot. Aside from their faces, the mere sight of which struck fear into people's hearts, and aside from the array of weapons they carried on their person—dagger, broadsword and blunderbuss (or flintlock, a rifle as big as a cannon)—they wore their hair gathered in a net that hid the great mass of locks which, when they wanted to make mischief, they would lower over their faces so that nobody could recognize them.

In short, to get an idea of what a bravo looked like, think of all the films about pirates you've ever seen. Compared to a bravo, all of Captain Hook's men seem like the little angels on the roof of a Nativity scene.

Now, the fearful priest we were talking about, whose name was Don Abbondio, was the vicar of a village on the beautiful shores of Lake Como. One evening, as he was quietly returning home, he came upon two bravoes who seemed clearly to be waiting for him. At the mere sight of them he was about to do what I said earlier, which for politeness' sake I won't repeat. Let's get right to the point, as the bravoes did. "Reverend," they said to him, "tomorrow you're supposed to marry that girl, Lucia Mondella, to that lad called Lorenzo or Renzo Tramaglino. Well, you mustn't marry them. If you do, something nasty might happen to you." There was no need for them to explain to Don Abbondio what might happen to him, because it was clear from the sharp teeth they revealed as they smiled like tigers that it would be something like a stabbing or a bullet, or both.

Don Abbondio tried to protest, but the bravoes let him know they had come at the behest of Don Rodrigo.

Don Rodrigo! Just hearing the name set Don Abbondio's blood racing and hands trembling. He was one of the petty nobles I was talking about, perhaps the worst of the lot, an overbearing, violent man. And why didn't Don Rodrigo want Renzo and Lucia to get married? Don Abbondio would find this out later, talking directly with Lucia, but for the moment he did not know. Don Rodrigo was a bully, someone who enjoyed lording it over people weaker than he. Like bullies nowadays who get bored straddling their motorcycles or scooters, he would harass the girls passing through the village on their way back from work at the silk mill. Don Rodrigo had bothered Lucia once—we can imagine with what crude compliments—and she had continued on her way, paying him no mind. And now Don Rodrigo wanted not only to avenge himself, but to prevent the girl from escaping his courtship and clutches through marriage.

So Don Abbondio goes home feeling as if he could die, and confides in his housekeeper, Perpetua. The good woman advises him to report the incident to the Archbishop of Milan, who was famous for being a protector of the poor and a righter of wrongs, but Don Abbondio is afraid even to do this. He has a hellish night, and the following morning, when Renzo shows up to iron out the last details of the marriage, the priest comes up with a string of incoherent excuses, overwhelms him with a stream of words in Latin that the poor young man can't make head or tail of, but in the end gets him to understand that, all things considered, it would be much better if he and Lucia did not get married.

Renzo was a good lad, but he had his difficult side, and he succeeded in making Perpetua talk, learning that behind the whole unpleasant matter was none other than Don Rodrigo. He runs to Lucia and her mother Agnese and tells them of the rascal's intrigues. Renzo was someone with not only a short fuse but also a dagger in his belt—like just about everyone else in those days—and he lets it be known that he would like to burst into Don Rodrigo's palace and commit a massacre. Imagine that, Renzo alone, who had never harmed a hair on anyone's head, against a gang of bravoes. He'd lost his mind.

Agnese succeeds in persuading him to go instead and seek the help of a powerful lawyer in the vicinity, a man so skilled in resolving the most intricate disputes that people called him the Pettifogger. And so he goes, bringing him two capons as a gift. At first Renzo has trouble explaining his predicament, and the lawyer, believing him to be a cut-throat like the others, is ready to help him avoid arrest, expressing himself in difficult words and Latin phrases to seem important. But when he realizes that Renzo is demanding justice against the most powerful noble in the area,

the Pettifogger chases him out of the house and even gives him back the two capons. He himself was counsel to Don Rodrigo, and one can imagine in what sordid affairs! And he didn't want any trouble with the powerful.

Two

Already from these first developments we can see the kind of story our good Signor Alessandro has started to tell: in this world there are the powerful, who are almost always bullies, and there are the little people, who have to put up with their tyranny. To keep the little people quiet, the powerful used either their cut-throats, who spoke the language of arms, or their counsellors, who, since the little people usually didn't know how to read or write, silenced them by confusing them with Latin—which at the time was not only the language of the Church, but also that of the law and of science in general.

And now we can breathe a sigh of relief, along with Signor Alessandro, who, as I said, was a good Christian—because, while some priests were fearful and cowardly, luckily there were others who were courageous. So our little people went and asked for the help of a certain Padre Cristoforo at the nearby monastery of Pescarenico.

This Cristoforo, when he was still called Lodovico, had himself been a profligate man-at-arms, of common birth but the son of a rich merchant, which allowed him to live the good life. He too engaged in acts of arrogance and bullying, until the day when he had an altercation over a matter that today seems laughable to us but at the time was grounds for a duel: that is, over a question of honour. To wit: if two men cross paths on the same pavement, who must step aside?

When Lodovico crossed paths with Signor So-and-So, the latter had said: "Out of the way!"

"No," Lodovico had replied, "you get out of the way, because I'm keeping to the right."

But Signor So-and-So said: "Oh, are you? But with people like you, the right always belongs to me!" Then, with insulting familiarity: "So step aside, craven mechanic, I'll show you how to behave towards a gentleman!"

"Craven mechanic, I?" Lodovico said under his breath, since at the time, calling anyone a mechanic—that is, a manual labourer—was a terrible insult when uttered by aristocrats who lived without working. And so he reacted. "You lie when you say I'm craven!" he said.

"No, you lie when you say I lie!"

And they went on in this fashion for a while, since these were the sorts of courtesies customarily exchanged before coming to blows or, as the case may be, before crossing swords. And if you think this sounds insane, well, it was; but if the noblemen of

those days could hear what two motorists say to each other nowadays when one dents the other's fender, they would say that *we* are insane.

At any rate, the seventeenth century isn't only the era in which many pirate films are set, but many films about musketeers as well. And so the two pull out their swords as their bravoes skirmish amongst themselves and people come running to see the show. When Signor So-and-So runs his blade through Cristoforo, Lodovico's old and faithful servant, Lodovico loses his head and lays his enemy out flat. He's killed a man!

At the time, to escape arrest, people usually took refuge in a church or a monastery, and Lodovico found asylum in a Capuchin monastery as the victim's entire family—brothers, cousins, relatives of every degree—circulated through the city looking for him, to avenge the affront. Not, mind you, for the grief felt over the death of a relative, but for the offence to their noble house.

At this point Lodovico decided to become a monk, taking on the name of his dead servant, Cristoforo. It wasn't, however, to escape the vendetta of his enemies, but rather because he felt genuinely crushed by remorse. To prove his courage, he fearlessly went straight to the palace of So-and-So's brother, who was waiting for him with all his relatives to enjoy the spectacle of his humiliation. Falling to his knees, Lodovico begged forgiveness with such humility, and real sorrow, that in the end the brother of the deceased and his relatives were moved. They embraced the penitent and realized that the best way to save their honour was to forgive. But what Signor Alessandro is trying to suggest to us (which he will do several times over the course of his story) is that it takes more courage to beg forgiveness—and to grant it—than to take revenge.

From that day on, Padre Cristoforo dedicated his life to defending the weak.

Three

Cristoforo therefore seemed the right man to go to Don Rodrigo and persuade him to leave Lucia alone. And so he went, but Don Rodrigo welcomed him with false courtesy at the table where he was dining with other nobles as well as, wouldn't you know it, the Pettifogger and the *podestà*, the man who should have put him in prison had the Pettifogger done his duty.

Then he treated the monk like a beggar and told him he didn't need a priest to preach morality to him. At this point

Cristoforo, with the look of someone who could still fight a duel, albeit without a sword, raised his right hand in a threatening gesture and placed his left on his hip, and shouted: "I'm not afraid of you and your ilk any more!", with insulting familiarity, as though Don Rodrigo were a craven mechanic himself. "Lucia will remain under the Lord's protection, but the same Lord's curse will fall upon this house!"

Rodrigo chased him away, hurling abuse at him, but since he had a dirty conscience, this business of God's curse would remain on his mind for ever after. And we shall see later that he would not lack the opportunity to remember it.

But while Padre Cristoforo's courage made up for the cowardice of Don Abbondio, he came away empty-handed.

If the two young people were already married, they could flee together and go somewhere else. In fact, just a stone's throw away, at Bergamo, the Duchy of Milan ended and the Republic of Venice began. But in those days, a boy and a girl who were not married could not run away together, because it would, at the very least, damage the girl's reputation for the rest of her life. To say nothing of a girl like Lucia, whom

Signor Alessandro portrays as strait-laced, all hearth and home, incapable of even looking at her fiancé without blushing, since she realizes she's in love with him but mustn't let it show because he's not yet her husband. Let's just say that it was a time when "respectable" girls didn't make a show of themselves in public in the company of boys, which should give you an idea of how times have changed.

Anyway, as Padre Cristoforo was looking for a way to help the two youngsters, both Renzo and Lucia as well as Don Rodrigo complicated matters for him. How?

On the one hand, Don Rodrigo summoned his top bravo, Griso, whose name alone inspired fear, and told him to round up a few henchmen and go that same night and kidnap Lucia from her home.

Renzo and Lucia, on the other hand, accepted the advice of Agnese, who had once heard it said that while the minister of Holy

Communion was the priest, and the minister of Confirmation was the bishop, the ministers of matrimony are the spouses themselves. That is, the priest declares them man and wife, but only after they have confirmed that this is their wish.

So Agnese suggested to them that they find a way to steal into Don Abbondio's room, appear suddenly in front of the priest, and declare that they want each other as husband and wife. At that point, with the priest as witness to their wishes, they would be good and married!

It turned out to be a rather muddled night. The betrothed stole into Don Abbondio's study and tried to say the famous words that would make them husband and wife, but Don Abbondio realized in time and upset his lamp and

table, ran to the window, and cried for help. The sacristan heard him and went and started ringing the tocsin. The entire village emptied out into the streets to see what was happening. Meanwhile, the bravoes entered Lucia's house but obviously found nobody there, and upon hearing the bells they thought that the alarm had been sounded and took to their heels in a confused retreat. Once the danger of that somewhat sneaky marriage had been averted, Don Abbondio tried to tell the villagers that there was nothing to be worried about, only a few vagabonds who had tried to break down his door. Some of the town folk believed this and others didn't, because in the meantime someone had seen a swarm of black-clad men racing out of Lucia's house and into the night... Total confusion, in short.

What's more, a manservant in Don Rodrigo's castle who was an honest person had got wind of his master's plans and alerted Padre Cristoforo, who had sent a boy to alert Renzo and Lucia. The boy found them as they were trying to sneak back home and warned them that there were bravoes there. The poor lovers immediately turned tail and took refuge with Padre Cristoforo.

And there something happened to make the betrothed's paths diverge. Cristoforo sent Lucia with a letter of introduction to the Capuchin convent in Monza, and Renzo with another letter for a certain Padre Bonaventura at the Milan monastery, beseeching him to find work for the young man there.

As a boat crossed the lake to take them far from a home they might never see again, Lucia glimpsed through the darkness the mountain tops in whose midst she had always lived, and the calm surface of the lake, and cried.

Four

Now the story gets more complicated. Is that possible? Yes. Renzo has to flee to Milan, while Lucia will be put up at the convent of cloistered nuns at Monza, under the special protection of the Lady. Except that for Lucia, meeting the Lady is like going from the frying pan into the fire, and Renzo happens to arrive in Milan at the very moment when a terrible uprising, or revolt, or maybe even a revolution, is in progress.

But let us proceed in orderly fashion. Who is the Lady? Don't forget what I said earlier about Don Abbondio: that in the seventeenth century many people became priests not by vocation but to find a way to live a quiet life without any troubles. But at least those like Don Abbondio had chosen their own destiny; there were others upon whom it was imposed against their will.

In the great families, as in all families in the past, people had a lot of children, but nobody wanted to share the inheritance. And so everything went to the eldest son: the title, the land, the houses, the castles and the rest of the wealth, while nothing went to the others. But how could they not give anything to the younger children? Simple: they would send the boys off to become friars and the girls to become nuns. Even if the children didn't want to do this? Well, yes.

The Lady of our story, whose name was Gertrude, was condemned to becoming a nun from the time she was a little girl. In fact, to get it into her head that this was her fate, she was only given dolls dressed up as nuns to play with, and everyone told her how happy and honoured she would be when she became an abbess, that is, a mother superior—because while all the nuns were equal, some, those from noble families, were more equal than the others and were assured the most important positions in the convent.

At the nuns' school there were also girls who would later return home and get married, and they, vain as all rich and spoilt young girls are, would tell each other of the beautiful clothes they would wear and the wonderful celebrations they would have. And Gertrude would eat her heart out.

She had indeed tried, at the last moment before taking her vows—when sent home to spend her final months with her family—to make her father understand that the prospect of being buried in a cloistered convent filled her with horror. But he'd treated her like a whimsical girl of easy virtue, ready to throw away a fine future, and told her she was breaking her parents' hearts. In short, she'd been properly brainwashed. And when, before the final moment, Gertrude had been questioned by a nice priest who was supposed to make sure that her choice was her own, she, sick at heart, had sworn that she wanted to become a nun of her own accord, and that no one had influenced her decision. The nice priest himself knew this wasn't true, it was written all over his face; but the seventeenth century was a very hypocritical age when appearance often mattered more than substance, and what one said was more important than what one did.

And so Gertrude became the Lady of the convent of Monza, locked for ever away inside those walls, never to come out again.

In the face of misfortune, some people resign themselves, while others get angry—like Renzo, for example, who wanted to do away with Don Rodrigo. Gertrude developed a cold resistance, secret and sullen, becoming despotic and cruel to her fellow nuns, and hating all the world.

Now, it just so happened that the window of her cell gave onto the garden of a certain Egidio, a wicked lord cut from the same cloth as Don Rodrigo, who had set his mind on seducing her. Gertrude was not made of the same stuff as Lucia and, truth be told, she had no Renzo waiting for her... And so she succumbed to his courtship. I don't know how they managed to get together; perhaps through some secret little door linking that wing of the convent with Egidio's garden. But, in short, they'd done what a nun should never do. Worse yet, when another young nun realized what was going on and started spreading gossip about it, Egidio, with Gertrude's complicitous silence, killed the girl and got rid of the corpse. Such was the nice new environment in which Lucia had ended up.

Gertrude had grown wicked because she'd been forced into the place by parents even more wicked than she, and we can certainly feel sorry for her and her ruined life, and many other things too. But the fact remains that it was in the hands of a wretch like her that Lucia's safety had been placed.

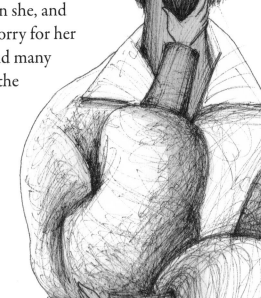

Five

Now another villain comes on the scene, by far the most wicked of all. He lived in the Alpine valleys nearby, perched high in an eagle's nest at the top of a mountain, with the access roads under the surveillance of squads of cut-throats armed to the teeth, a petty lord so fierce that people were afraid even to utter his name. Not even Signor Alessandro, our author, dared say it, and so we know him only as the Unnameable.

This Unnameable was not only a rake and a scoundrel like Don Rodrigo; he was a proper criminal who broke every law, lent aid to despots like himself, and committed crimes, I would say, just for the pleasure of being wicked. I couldn't tell you exactly how many or what kind of misdeeds they were, but you should imagine him as the equivalent of someone associated with the Mafia or the Camorra today, who deals drugs and runs a kidnapping ring. On top of this, he bought off judges and government officials (who were very corrupt in those days), so that nobody would ever have dared to put him in jail. Is that bad enough for you?

And since people like that are made for each other, the Unnameable was a friend of Don Rodrigo, who respected and feared him. Meanwhile Don Rodrigo, who couldn't quite swallow the fact that Lucia had slipped his grasp, had done three things. First, he'd succeeded in picking up Lucia's trail all the way to Monza. Second, to rid himself of Padre Cristoforo, the only person who could still make trouble for him, he'd appealed to a very powerful uncle of his who was highly influential, even with the Capuchins, and managed to get Padre Cristoforo transferred to Rimini—which, with the sort of transportation they had in those days, when everyone except the nobility travelled on foot and there was no postal service, was like having him banished to another continent. Third, he'd gone personally to the Unnameable and asked a small favour of him: to kidnap Lucia and turn her over to him.

And, wouldn't you know it, the Unnameable was in turn a friend of Egidio's (since rogues like to help one another); add to this the evil powers that Egidio had over the Lady, and you can draw your own conclusions.

Though in despair at having to do something so wicked to Lucia, whom she'd almost grown fond of, the Lady could not or would not disobey her

perfidious friend. She pretended to give Lucia an assignment, sending her to the Capuchin monastery to deliver a message. On her way there Lucia saw a carriage, but did not manage in time to see the sinister faces inside it before the Unnameable's bravoes, under the command of the fearsome Nibbio ("the Buzzard"), seized her, locked her inside the vehicle and took her up to the castle.

Six

You'll have to excuse me for skipping from one thing to another, but this is a story of many misfortunes, and now we must concern ourselves with what has been happening in the meantime to Renzo, who arrived in Milan just as a desperate mob had started attacking the bread ovens.

What had happened? All of Piedmont and Lombardy at the time were involved in what came to be known as the Thirty Years' War, though it was only called that afterwards, since at the start nobody knew that it would last so long.

Don't try to understand what was going on, because it was one big mess, as we might say today, with the Spanish and the Germans fighting the French, the Duke of Savoy not knowing whose side he was on, the city of Casale Monferrato under siege, and Mantua defeated and sacked.

In those days, a war was fought primarily by mercenaries, men who lived by fighting for whoever would pay them, but they would fight even without pay, so long as they had licence to plunder. When they entered a city they would put all the inhabitants to the sword and empty out every house, church and palace. Thus, wherever they passed, it was as though plagues of locusts had passed through, and it didn't matter whether the territory they crossed was friendly or belonged to the enemy—they would devour everything. They were bloodthirsty by trade, and almost always drunk.

Clearly, a country at war—crawling with these hordes of scoundrels, with leaders thinking only of spending on weapons without figuring whether they had enough money and foodstuffs, with crops gone to ruin under the marching feet of armies—could not help but suffer an economic crisis, a lack of basic needs, and all-out famine.

This was why the Milanese took to the streets over the price of bread. Bread first and foremost, because only once in a while did the poor have anything to eat along with their bread, and so bread was the primary food source.

For a moment there was no bread at all to be had, and then, to calm people down, the government put bread at such a derisory price that it was sure to ruin the bakers; then the price was raised again, but by now the people were in a rage... In short, at a certain point the throngs couldn't stand it any longer and started plundering the bread ovens.

In so doing, they wasted more bread and flour than they could ever have eaten. The attackers seized sacks overflowing with flour that spilt along the streets; others made off with baskets so full of bread that a third of it fell out as they ran. This was why when Renzo entered the city he saw white streaks and loaves scattered here and there on the ground, as if he were in the Land of Plenty.

Since he was hungry, he didn't deny himself two nice loaves of bread. But since he was also an honest lad, he'd promised himself to pay for them if he could ever find their rightful owner. Imagine that, amidst all the bedlam. And when he didn't find the Padre Bonaventura he was supposed to meet at the monastery, he'd started wandering about the city. He heard talk of protests and injustices and, amidst that mob of hotheads, got a little worked up himself. Hearing everyone demanding justice over the bread crisis, all he could think of was the injustice

he had suffered at the hands of Don Rodrigo, and so he started preaching about the need to punish scoundrels and respect the rights of the poor. But, to anyone who listened to him, he sounded like someone trying to incite the people against the government.

Or so it seemed, at least, to a police informer whose job it was to go back, at the end of each day, and identify a few guilty parties amidst the throng of guilty parties, so that they could be duly hanged in the coming days to set an example.

That's what the death penalty is for. You don't kill to punish someone who has done wrong, but to send a warning to anyone who might be thinking of doing the same in the future. Therefore it doesn't really matter whether the person put to death is actually guilty, or more guilty than anyone else. And if you don't like this way of administering justice, you should know that there are many countries today which still do it this way.

And so Renzo seemed like the perfect fall guy, since, on top of everything else, when the spy followed him into a tavern, our young protagonist started drinking more than he was accustomed to—in a word, he got drunk and, as often happens to people when they're drunk, he started blustering and griping, calling for due punishment of all the wicked, and he blurted out his name... In short, the informer went and delivered his report, and the following morning a couple of gendarmes and a police inspector came and arrested him.

The city, however, was still in uproar. Patrols of insurgents circulated freely, and the gendarmes were more afraid than the people they were arresting. Renzo, who by now had recovered from the wine's effects, understood the situation and started shouting: "Friends, they're taking me to prison because yesterday like you I demanded bread and justice!"

The throng was moved and surrounded the gendarmes, who blanched in terror and wished only that they were somewhere else. And, indeed, they took to their heels, leaving Renzo free to run away as if he had wings on his feet.

Renzo managed to leave the city. His only thought was to reach the River Adda, where the Duchy of Milan ended and the Republic of Venice began. But he was afraid to ask for directions, and when he stopped at an inn he overheard a merchant coming from Milan say that everyone was looking for a terrible rapscallion from out of town who was going around exhorting the people to kill all the nobles. ("And how would the poor get by if all the nobles were killed?" the merchant whined, since, in his line of work, he felt more at ease with the rich than the poor.) The gendarmes, moreover, had found in this outsider's pocket a bundle of letters (which in fact was only the letter that Padre Cristoforo had given him to present to Padre Bonaventura!), proof that he'd been sent by who-knows-who to fan the flames of revolt and so on and so forth.

Thus terrified, and henceforth banished from Milan and in danger of being hanged if he were ever caught, Renzo, after myriad trials and troubles, arrived at last in the province of Bergamo, where his cousin Bortolo found him a good job. We'll leave him there for now, and return to the story of the unhappy Lucia.

Seven

Here we'll pick up what happened that same evening and night to both Lucia and the Unnameable—since you will have noticed by now that Signor Alessandro tells his stories as though they were parts of a film, following several characters at once, showing us one and then going back to let us see what the other was doing in the meantime.

Lucia is taken up the steep path leading to the eagle's nest, feeling more and more terrified, imploring her kidnappers to release her. So touching is her distress that Nibbio, who was rather hard-hearted, after all, and used to doing the wickedest sorts of things, very nearly takes pity on her.

From a castle window the Unnameable sees the carriage with his prey in it and has a strange feeling, as if realizing that what he is doing is wrong. How could this be, with a man like that?

When he goes to see Lucia, she throws herself at his feet and beseeches him to free her, saying something he has never heard before in his life: "God forgives many things for an act of mercy!"

The Unnameable steps back, promising not to harm her and postponing the whole matter until the following morning. Lucia spends a night of terror and anguish and, not knowing whom to turn to, makes a vow to the Blessed Virgin: if she is freed from that torment, she will no longer get married and will devote her life instead to her, the Virgin Mary.

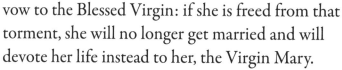

The Unnameable, however, had an even more frightful night, troubled as he was by seeing Lucia. The girl, who just now seemed to us a limpid spring, a little saint, a young peasant lass all hearth and home, pretty perhaps, but a bit uncouth, must actually have possessed great charm, combining innocence, sweetness and delicacy (and perhaps real beauty), if she could inspire such noble sentiments in a soul so corrupt. And indeed that man with a heart of stone began to feel pity and remorse.

If this seems unrealistic, we must bear in mind that Signor Alessandro is trying to tell us something through his story. People certainly become wicked or cowardly due to circumstances and the ways of the world: Don Abbondio became a priest without a calling because the poor were given few alternatives to improve their lot; Gertrude became wicked because the laws of succession were what they were, and her parents and family were "children of their time"; Don Rodrigo was a scoundrel because a society based on privilege had made him that way; and quite possibly the bravoes had become thugs because they were driven to it by poverty. But people aren't shaped by external circumstances alone. They have moral awareness, are responsible for their actions, and hear the voice of their conscience. If these characters had the strength to listen to their conscience, Don Abbondio would not behave like a coward, Gertrude like a criminal, or Rodrigo like a prevaricator. And the proof of this is that the Unnameable is able to listen to the voice of his conscience.

At once he realizes that his life of crime has been pointless and meaningless. Then he notices that, down in the valley, all the people are gathering festively in a nearby village to see the archbishop of Milan, Cardinal Federigo Borromeo, who everyone says will be made a saint. "What has that man got that makes all those people so happy?" the Unnameable wonders. And so, driven by an impulse that he himself can't explain, he decides to go and see him too.

It's true that this conversion seems a bit sudden, I'll grant you that. But Signor Alessandro had faith in miracles, and if we don't believe in miracles, we should at least consider this transformation as having been long percolating in the Unnameable's heart without his realizing it.

In short, the scoundrel goes straight to the Cardinal; and the moment he enters the building with his broadsword, dagger and pistols in his belt, and his rifle slung

across his shoulders, all the parish priests there to pay homage to their archbishop make the sign of the Cross, trembling from head to toe. The Cardinal, however, upon learning that the man wishes to see him, replies at once that he should be let in, and welcomes him with great joy and affection, as if he already knew (and perhaps that devil of a saint already did know) that he had come to confess his sins and to declare that from now on he would devote himself to atoning for all the bad he'd done.

And so it was. The Unnameable becomes unblameable (sorry about that) by virtue of divine grace, and the first thing he does is to explain to the Cardinal the terrible thing he's done to Lucia. And so, with the Cardinal's blessing, he prepares to return to his castle to free her. Among the parish priests waiting in the next room, the Cardinal flushes out Don Abbondio to accompany the Unnameable, so the girl can see at least one friendly face. Or that, at least, was what the Cardinal thought, not knowing yet whose side Don Abbondio was on in the whole affair. When later he learns from Lucia and her mother how the priest has behaved, he gives him a dressing-down of the kind that makes you want to disappear. "What?" he says, "You didn't know that a priest must know how to sacrifice himself for the good of his congregation? Didn't it occur to you to come and inform me of the threats that were made? Weren't you ever taught that the habit you wear demands devotion, sacrifice and courage?"

Right. Meanwhile Don Abbondio was muttering to himself, "Oh, sure, it's easy enough for a saint to say. After all, he's not the one who'll get shot in the belly by the bravoes. If this holy man could only stand in my shoes... I got a good look at those ugly faces, not him... And then he goes and throws his arms around that hell-raiser, while with me he makes a big scene for a little white lie I told to save my skin..."

Naturally, he didn't really say these things, but in fact apologized, said he'd probably been wrong, and bowed his head. Someone who was afraid of everything would certainly be afraid of a Cardinal as well. But later, after he returned home, he lived for months in the fear that the betrothed couple would come back to ask him to marry them again, while Don Rodrigo was still there in his wicked palace, ready to send his bravoes again. In short, the priest was a chickenshit, and would for ever remain a chickenshit.

So we can only imagine him that morning, when the Cardinal sent him on a mission to that accursed castle in the company of a cut-throat whose conversion hadn't convinced him one bit. He climbed the mountain trembling like a leaf, wildly terrified that the man might suddenly change his mind and become wicked again as before.

Eight

At any rate, the expedition went well. Lucia was now free, her mother Agnese came to be with her, and the Unnameable gave her a dowry of 100 gold *scudi*. The two little women had never seen so much money before.

Since it would be too dangerous to return to the village, Lucia is taken on as a lady-in-waiting to a certain Donna Prassede. In the meantime they get news that Renzo has disappeared beyond the border, wanted for activities that today we would call terroristic; and the longer he was out of sight, the more the rumours flew, to the point where it began to seem as if he was organizing the upheaval in Milan all by himself. For this reason, Donna Prassede resolved to convince the good Lucia not to think any more about a troublemaker like that. Lucia defended her beloved, but she realized that now, because of her vow, she could no longer love him and would have to forget about him in earnest. In despair, she told her mother everything.

Agnese managed to track down Renzo and write to him, sending him half of the dowry given by the Unnameable, almost as a kind of consolation prize, and telling him about Lucia's vow. Agnese, however, didn't know how to write, and had dictated the letter to someone who could understand only so much of the story and set it down as best he could. The letter reached Renzo, who didn't know how to read, and the person who read it to him, not understanding a great deal of what Agnese was saying, interpreted it as best he could, guaranteeing that Renzo would understand even less. All the poor lad was able to surmise was that Lucia didn't want anything more to do with him. And he despaired and wondered why. He would have liked to go back to Milan to clear things up, but was afraid of getting arrested.

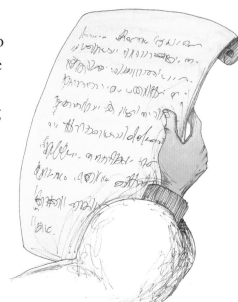

By this point, in short, the situation is even more drastic than before when, suddenly, the plot thickens and... (drumroll) the plague hits! Actually, that should be the Plague, with a capital P, a scourge of immense proportions.

It could not have been otherwise. Thousands
and thousands of mercenary soldiers, all filthy
and full of infections, passing through towns and
countrysides, doing their business by the side of the
road, bloody clashes whose victims lay dead on the
ground, with nobody bothering to bury them—
these were ideal conditions for pestilence to spread.
Of course the disease would not have spread quite
so fast had people been more concerned and taken
all the necessary hygienic precautions. But in those
days hygiene was what it was. Only later did a few
scientists—whom nobody listened to anyway—
formulate the hypothesis that plagues were caused by
tiny little animals called germs.

The very idea of plague, moreover, aroused such
fear that, at least at first, the initial concern, not
only of the common people but of the authorities
themselves, was to deny its existence. When the
corpses began to appear, people said that it was due
to swamp fever. Then other testimonies began to
emerge, but the governor of Milan had the ongoing
war to worry about and couldn't be bothered with a
pesky little fever. Finally somebody saw the first bubo,
the bluish boil that would usually appear in a person's

armpit. This was a sure sign of plague. In terror, the authorities proclaimed the need for a large procession of citizens to pray for divine intervention, without even imagining that bringing thousands of people together, in close contact with one another, was the best way to spread the disease. And, as if this wasn't enough, even when confronted with the buboes, the stupidest doctors spoke not of plague but of "pestilential fever". As though by changing the word they changed the thing itself.

You have to realize—and Signor Alessandro makes this very clear—that when things go wrong, it is often the fault of bad people, but it is even more often the fault of stupid people.

When no one could any longer deny the existence of the plague, and people were dropping dead in the streets, all of Lombardy sort of went mad. Unable to deny the terrible reality any more, people started wondering whom to blame. *We* are to blame, every one of them should have said. As was anyone who did not immediately recognize the disease, who delayed preparing defences, care and disinfection. But it's always hard to say "It's my fault." And so rumours of plague-sowers began to spread. That is, people began to think that some evil-doers, possibly enemy agents, or sent by the devil, were going around spreading poisons carrying plague germs on walls, doors and everywhere.

So as more and more people started dying, and the *lazzaretto*, the hospital for plague victims, was filled to bursting, everyone began looking out for the accursed plague-sowers. Some thought they'd seen a person smearing something on benches in the cathedral and brought the benches outside onto the parvis to clean them; but when people saw that pile of wood they started saying that all the benches in the cathedral had been tainted. One morning some yellowish goo had been discovered on many doors and walls. Maybe it was a sick joke, or, more likely, those walls and doors had long been dirty and nobody had ever noticed. By now, however, a collective madness had taken hold, and anyone whose clothes made them look foreign was

considered a plague-sower. It is always easier, after all,
to hate an outsider than your next-door neighbour.
An old man was lynched for dusting off a bench.
If someone on the street took off his hat to ask for
directions, people started screaming that he had
poisonous powder hidden in the brim to scatter on
the victim. One man had touched the façade of the
cathedral to feel the texture of the stone, and an
enraged mob set upon him.

To add to the terror, the city was crawling with
monatti, the red-clad corpse-bearers who went
around collecting the dead bodies to take them to the
communal graves, and whose strategy for protecting

themselves from contagion was to drink non-stop. Thus, perpetually drunk, they passed through the city on their carts, sitting atop mountains of corpses, imbued with the stench of death, plundering the homes of the sick they came to take away, sometimes when still alive. It was said that they helped to spread the contagion by throwing the rags of the plague victims onto the street, since by now the pestilence had become their source of income.

Nine

In short, there were hair-raising scenes all around. Every family had its dead and dying, and it was into this desolate setting that Renzo reappeared. He had contracted the plague, but had recovered because he was a hardy young man, and from that moment on he could no longer be infected with it again. He'd figured that with all that was going on, nobody would bother with him any more, and he was right. The authorities had far bigger concerns on their minds. And so he'd decided to return to Milan. To find Lucia, naturally, with whom he'd fallen completely out of touch.

Thinking she might be at Donna Prassede's house, he went there. A woman came to the window and told him rudely that Lucia had been taken to the *lazzaretto*. Then, seeing that he kept knocking at the door, anxious as he was for more information, she started shouting: "Stop the plague-sower!" People in those days were utterly terrified, we must realize. They'd sort of lost their minds.

Renzo escaped from the enraged mob by jumping onto a cart full of corpses and wine-swilling *monatti*, who at first thought he really was a plague-sower, and then someone who gathered the sick for them. They then realized that he was just a poor youth and started calling him a two-bit little plague-sower.

Renzo fled in disgust from this riff-raff and finally made it to the *lazzaretto*, where he now wandered about, lost, wondering how he would ever find Lucia alive or dead amidst all that filth and confusion.

Then, all at once, as if by miracle, in a cabin doorway he spots Padre Cristoforo, who at the first mention of plague had obtained permission to return to Lombardy to help care for the sick. And he had done so without sparing himself, Renzo painfully realized, as the

monk's face bore the signs of the disease, which was devouring him.

Padre Cristoforo had entirely lost touch with Renzo and Lucia after his transfer, and Renzo too had little idea of the many things that had happened to his fiancée in the meantime. In despair the youth merely says to Padre Cristoforo that if he doesn't find her alive, "he'll know exactly what to do". And from the look in the young man's eye, Padre Cristoforo realizes that Renzo is contemplating revenge against Don Rodrigo. And so he grabs him by the arm sternly, almost angrily, and takes him into the cabin.

In the back, almost unrecognizable from the pustules covering his face, lies Don Rodrigo, dying.

He'd noticed one night, when returning from an evening of revelry with his friends, that he had a terrible boil. Terrified that he'd be taken to a *lazzaretto*, he had instructed Griso, reminding him of all the benefits he'd lavished upon him, to go and find, on the sly, an obliging doctor. Shortly afterwards, however, two *monatti* came into his house, and he realized that Griso, a servant worthy of his master, had betrayed him and was already breaking into his coffers to divvy up the money with the two red-clad men carrying him away as if he were already a corpse. Griso, incidentally, would himself die shortly thereafter, having touched his master's clothes in the hope of finding still more valuables. But we won't trouble ourselves over his fate, since he got what he deserved.

Padre Cristoforo shows Don Rodrigo to Renzo as if to say: "See how the Lord has already punished this wretch, without waiting for you? So forget your rage and hatred, and find it in your heart to forgive this dying man."

So Renzo forgives him. Now free of hatred (because hatred is a great burden), he wanders about the *lazzaretto*, looking for Lucia. And, lo and behold, another miracle! He finds her, returned to health, in a cabin, helping another sick woman on the road to recovery.

Lucia feels great joy upon seeing him, then remembers her vow and withdraws. Renzo shouts to her that she had no right to make a vow that involved him as well. In despair Lucia says that she can't go back, and Renzo drags her into Padre Cristoforo's cabin. Here the good monk explains to Lucia what Renzo, though a coarse highlander, has well understood, rendered wise by his love. "You cannot," he says, "make a vow in the name of another person. You, Lucia, could certainly have decided never to get married, but not after you promised yourself to Renzo. And so, by the power vested in me by the Church as its vicar, I can release you from your vow. If you so wish, and if you ask me to do so."

This last statement Padre Cristoforo said with benevolent guile. In other words, he was asking Lucia: "If not for your vow, would you have any reason not to marry Renzo?"

And Lucia, despite her modesty, and with all the shyness that had led us to believe she was a little saint incapable of great passion, immediately replies that she has no other reason, and lets it be known, albeit through a great deal of blushing, that she is dying to marry Renzo.

What else is there to say? All's well that ends well. Padre Cristoforo takes his leave of the two young lovers, who know perfectly well they'll never see him again on this earth. They return to their village and

reunite with Agnese. Don Abbondio still hesitates to join them in marriage until he's certain that Don Rodrigo is really dead, and he isn't fully convinced until Rodrigo's heir takes up residence in his palace. This heir, moreover, turns out to be a very fine fellow and even holds a grand wedding banquet for the couple.

Renzo and Lucia then move for good with Agnese to the province of Bergamo, where Renzo eventually sets up a small silk mill all his own, and they do not fail to bring a large brood of children into the world, all grandchildren of Agnese, who loves to kiss them so hard on the cheeks it always leaves a mark.

Our story should end here, except for the fact that a question arises. Or rather, a question arises for me, the person telling this story, and I would like to address it to Signor Alessandro, the person who told me the story. But it should also concern you, who are reading me, provided you weren't bored by the story.

Epilogue

The question is this: What is the point of this story? While it's true that there are stories without any point at all, a story as long and complicated as this one should have a moral, considering that even fables, which are very short, have morals. Why did Signor Alessandro want to tell us this tale?

If we think hard about what he told us, it seems clear that Signor Alessandro is on the side of the poor, who always suffer injustices, and he doesn't go easy on the wicked. And the same is true for us, I think. Were there any of you who rooted for Don Rodrigo to win the battle?

Still, almost up to the end, the poor seemed on the verge of losing. True, the Cardinal boarded Lucia with a fine lady, and the Unnameable even gave her a dowry. But Lucia still couldn't go back home, where Don Rodrigo was waiting for her like a vulture lurking in a tree; Don Abbondio was still scared to death despite the Cardinal's tirade; Renzo remained an exile in the Republic of Venice; and in any case Lucia could no longer marry him.

In short, except for the Unnameable, who had become good, the bad guys were still doing fine, while the good guys, poor things, hadn't even managed to change their condition through an uprising, because the uprising was put down, four wretches were hanged, and the bosses remained the bosses. Signor Alessandro seems to love the poor very much, but clearly he has no idea how to help them assert their rights. And since he was in fact a rather fervent Christian, everyone has always said that the moral of his story is that we must resign ourselves and put our only hope in Providence.

And, indeed, in the end Providence arrives. But in the guise of the plague.

The plague is like a broom that sweeps away all the dirt. It kills Don Rodrigo and Griso, brings peace to Don Abbondio, makes everyone forget the uprising so that nobody is concerned any more with looking for Renzo, brings Renzo and Lucia back together, and so on and so forth. In short, it all turns out well, but at what a cost! This providential plague kills off two-thirds of the population of Milan, dispatches to the next world (even if this means Heaven) Padre Cristoforo and many other good people who had nothing to do with anything. And while Renzo and Lucia should thank the plague for having helped them, they should also admit that Providence is a terrible force that looks nobody in the eye and sometimes casts the good and bad into the same grave.

I don't believe Signor Alessandro thought of Providence as brutal, but it's clear he wasn't an optimist. He believed in Providence, but knew that life is hard and cruel, and Providence can be a consolation, or it can cause great distress. And since it can't make everyone happy, it does what it does according to plans that are beyond our ken.

And so, by urging us to have faith in Providence, Signor Alessandro in fact limits himself to advising us to love the defenceless, and to do as the good people in the story did and help them. "You see," he seems to be saying, "even if the world is not a nice place, and I have concealed none of its ugliness, drama, sorrow, and death; if people could just have a little more compassion for their fellow man, this world would appear a little—even if only a little—less ugly."

The story doesn't teach us any more than this. And Signor Alessandro doesn't say any more than this. And that, perhaps, is why, as I told you at the beginning, he had a face that looked like a good, sad horse.

This book is dedicated to Pietro.

WHERE IS THIS STORY FROM?

Some grown-ups, seeing you reading this story, will probably tell you to stop and not read *The Betrothed*, the real book written by Alessandro Manzoni, because it's a crashing bore and unreadable. Don't listen to them. Many think *The Betrothed* is boring because they were forced to read it in school around the age of fourteen, and everything we do because we're forced to do it is tedious. I chose to tell you this story because my dad had given me the book before I had to read it in school, and so I enjoyed it as much as I did the adventure novels I was reading at the time. Of course it was more demanding, some of the descriptions are a little long and one doesn't really begin to savour them until the second or third reading, but, I assure you, it's an exciting book. I don't know whether kids are still made to read the book in school nowadays; if you're lucky enough not to have to study it, try reading it on your own when you're a little older. It's worth the trouble.

Alessandro Manzoni took twenty years to write this book. He started in 1821 (almost 200 years ago, imagine that) and finished in 1840. The first version appeared in 1823, as *Fermo and Lucia*. But Manzoni wasn't satisfied with it and started rewriting the novel, which was published as *The Betrothed* in 1827. Yet, once again, despite the book's great success, Manzoni still wasn't happy. It took him another twelve years before the definitive edition came out between 1840 and 1842, accompanied by beautiful illustrations that Manzoni discussed one by one with the artist, Francesco Gonin.

For that edition Manzoni had wanted to improve the language, drawing his inspiration from the Italian spoken in Florence (he said he "rinsed his clothes in the River Arno"), so that he would be understood clearly by all Italians, who at the time spoke many different forms of Italian.

But there were also economic reasons for this edition. At the time, in fact, royalties laws were vague—that is, the law whereby the author of a book is protected by contract and collects at least ten per cent of the proceeds for every copy sold. If somebody republishes the book without telling the author, and without giving him a penny, we have what is called a pirate edition.

Well, the 1827 edition was so successful that eight pirate editions were published that same year, and within ten years no less than seventy existed, to say nothing of the translations into other languages. Imagine that: seventy pirate editions, hordes of people reading the book and saying, "This Manzoni is really good!" and meanwhile poor Manzoni himself didn't see a penny.

And so Manzoni said to himself: "I'm going to bring out a new edition, publish one instalment every week, with illustrations that will be difficult to copy. That'll show those pirates!"

Not a chance. A Naples publisher managed to bring out pirated instalments at almost the same time as the originals, and once again Manzoni, who had had a great many copies printed, not only didn't earn anything, but had actually paid for the publishing costs. Good thing he was from a prosperous family. Even if he wasn't rich, he certainly wasn't dying of starvation.

So why did Manzoni, who until then had written beautiful poetry and dramas in verse, devote so much time to this story, which seemed a pretty humdrum tale about an engaged couple who have trouble getting married but in the end manage to come out all right? And why write a story that takes place in the 1600s, that is, a time remote not only from us but even from the readers of his time? Manzoni, however, was not only a great writer but a patriot. Italy was still divided at the time, and the Lombardy in which he lived was under Austrian rule. Those were the years of the Risorgimento, the Italian struggle for independence, which culminated in the unification of the country, an event whose 150th anniversary we recently celebrated here. And Manzoni, in telling the story of a Lombardy under foreign domination (at the time of his story, the foreign rulers were Spanish, not Austrian), was describing events that his readers would find rather similar to their own experiences.

This explains in part the book's success, but it's not clear why foreign readers liked it so much, or why the story has since been retold so many times in other mediums such as film, television and even comic books. The reason is that it's a good story, there's no getting around it.

When you read the book you'll also see that Manzoni claims to be copying it from an antique notebook he discovered by chance. It's a device used by many novelists, to give the impression that they're telling a true story. But in fact it was later discovered that many of the characters featured in the novel, from the nun of Monza to the Unnameable, not to mention Cardinal Federigo and others, had actually existed.

Finally, *The Betrothed* remains important to Italian readers because the novels written in Italy over the two previous centuries were not of very high quality, whereas in France, England and Germany people had been writing great novels. Manzoni's book was the first great Italian novel and a major influence on all the writers who came after him. Even those who found it boring.

U.E.

UMBERTO ECO has taught in many universities and written some very difficult books for his students, which you will probably never read, but that's not the end of the world. He has also written six novels (the most famous being *The Name of the Rose*), which have made him one of the best-known living Italian writers in all the world. He has received forty honorary degrees from universities in a great number of countries—the kind of degrees that luckily you don't have to study for, but which they grant you because they like what you've written. Nobody, however, has ever read his first story, which he wrote when he was ten years old. You should try writing one yourself sometime.

MARCO LORENZETTI was born in the Italian region of Marche. He has loved drawing since he was a child, and at school his favourite subjects were Art, History and Mythology. In 2010 he attained a "Master Ars in Fabula" in Illustration from Macerata. For "Save the Story" he has also illustrated *The Story of Gilgamesh* by Yiyun Li. He lives and works in Ancona.

STEPHEN SARTARELLI is an award-winning translator and poet. He has translated more than thirty books from Italian and French and has published three volumes and numerous chapbooks of poetry. He lives in France.

SAVE THE STORY is a library of favourite stories from around the world, retold for today's children by some of the best contemporary writers. The stories they retell span cultures (from Ancient Greece to nineteenth-century Russia), time and genres (from comedy and romance to mythology and the realist novel), and they have inspired all manner of artists for many generations.

Save the Story is a mission in book form: saving great stories from oblivion by retelling them for a new, younger generation.

THE HOLDEN SCHOOL (www.scuolaholden.it) was founded in Turin in 1994 with the idea of creating something unique, and is open to students from all over the world. It looks a lot like a huge house with no lack of space, books and coffee. People study something called "storytelling" there—that is, the secret of telling stories in every possible language: literature, film, television, theatre, comics—all of it with the most outlandish results.

This series is dedicated to Achille, Aglaia, Arturo, Clara, Kostas, Olivia, Pietro, Samuele, Sandra, Sebastiano and Sofia.

PUSHKIN CHILDREN'S BOOKS

Just as we all are, children are fascinated by stories. From the earliest age, we love to hear about monsters and heroes, romance and death, disaster and rescue, from every place and time.

In 2013, we created Pushkin Children's Books to share these tales from different languages and cultures with younger readers, and to open the door to the wide, colourful worlds these stories offer.

From picture books and adventure stories to fairy tales and classics, and from fifty-year-old bestsellers to current huge successes abroad, the books on the Pushkin Children's list reflect the very best stories from around the world, for our most discerning readers of all: children.

For more great stories, visit www.pushkinchildrens.com

SAVE THE STORY: THE SERIES

Don Juan by Alessandro Baricco

Cyrano de Bergerac by Stefano Benni

The Nose by Andrea Camilleri

Gulliver by Jonathan Coe

The Betrothed by Umberto Eco

Captain Nemo by Dave Eggers

Gilgamesh by Yiyun Li

King Lear by Melania G. Mazzucco

Antigone by Ali Smith

Crime and Punishment by A. B. Yehoshua